Some Kind
of Ride

Stories & Drawings
For Making Sense of It All

StoryPeople
Decorah

ISBN-13: 978-0-974551-60-9
ISBN-10: 0-9745516-0-0

The people in this book, if at one time real, are now entirely fictitious, having been subjected to a combination of a selective memory and a fertile imagination. Any resemblance to real people you might know, even if they are the author's relatives, is entirely coincidental, and is a reminder that you are imagining the incidents in this book as much as the author. (By the way, the "she" is not who you think it is, either. So, give it up...)

StoryPeople
P.O. Box 7
Decorah, IA 52101
USA
563.382.8060
563.382.0263 FAX
800.476.7178

storypeople@storypeople.com
www.storypeople.com

First Edition: *September, 2006*

*Produced by O'Brien & Whitaker, Oakland, California
on 30% post-consumer fiber archival text paper*

To my sons, for their laughter & wisdom &
breathtakingly exuberant trust in life

& always, to my dearest Ellen, for seeing all
that is good & true in the heart of the world.

I truly can't imagine the ride without you all...

Other books by Brian Andreas available
from StoryPeople Press:

Mostly True
Still Mostly True
Going Somewhere Soon
Strange Dreams
Hearing Voices
Story People
Trusting Soul
Traveling Light

Some Kind of Ride

Introduction

I have to admit that I actually thought about how big a typeface I could get away with in this introduction. By the time I'd finished the book, I was pretty much done talking. At one point I asked Ellen if she thought anyone would notice if I used 48 point text, which would give me about 15 words per page. She wisely ignored me.

Last year, I actually stopped writing stories. I felt like I didn't have anything more to say in words, so one morning I went to the art store & came back with a carload of canvases & started painting. For six months I painted & wrote nothing. Then, one morning, the words decided it was time to return. It was like beginning again.

So, when it came time to start this new book, I felt a little raw & unsure of how it would go. I knew how to do a book the old way, but this new way was speaking to me in dreams & leading me deep into places I'd never been. It felt like I was being called to remember something important. Even now, with it complete in front of me on my desk, I still feel not quite returned from the far-off places I went.

That's why I can't tell you what it means yet.

These stories & paintings & drawings feel like the visible ripples of a much deeper conversation. There are whispers of death & rebirth, spinning their threads throughout the stories. There are echoes of ancient tricksters in the voices of modern teenagers. There is bawdy, irrepressible laughter & a thin, keening sadness for worlds lost. Yet, beneath it all, there is a true wonder & love for this world. These stories talk among themselves in a way that I haven't seen in the other books & there are threads woven between them so finely that I haven't yet followed them to their source.

It's almost like these stories hold a key to making sense of this new world that's in the process of being born. It is a messy & ungainly, beautiful & incoherent thing. Still, it is the only world we have & we're the only people to make it work. We may not be the best choice for the job, but we're the ones who are here. Perhaps, in the end, that's what this book is supposed to mean. Here are stories to remind you that you're alive & filled with every possibility the universe can imagine. Stories to remind you that life is yours to make into a wonder of love & adventure & connection. Stories to remind you that every story matters, now more than ever.

There is not much more to say. Everything you need here, you will find. Pay attention. Hold the world gently. Blessings on you & on all you hold dear. Above all, remember always through the coming years, that while it may feel like some kind of ride, it really is just life, going absolutely perfectly.

With love,

Brian Andreas
On Matthew's birthday
16 October 2006

**feels like
some kind of ride
but it's turning out
just to be life
going absolutely
perfectly**

Some Kind of Ride

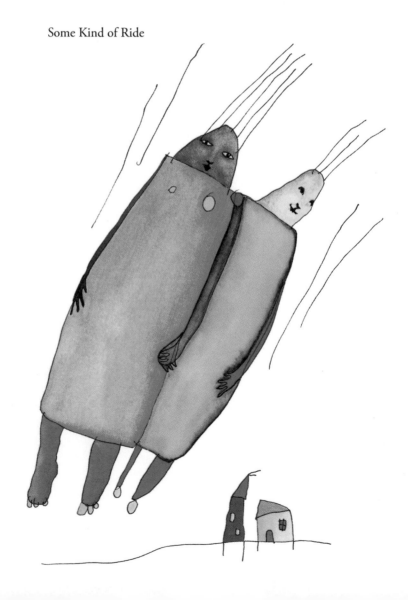

Remember to use positive affirmations.

I am not a dork is not one of them.

Positive Affirmations

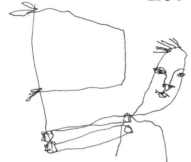

When I grow up,
he said, I want
to be just like you,
except for the hairs in
your ears & nose.

That's too gross,
he explained.

Gross Anatomy

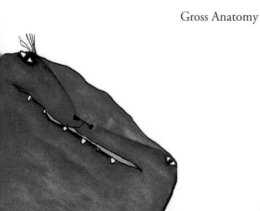

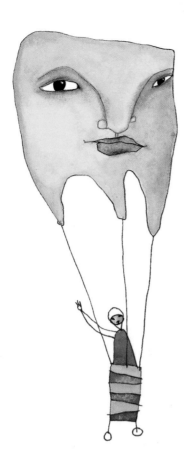

this is the center
of the universe
at this moment
unless you're
looking in another
direction, or are
thinking about
something from
a long time ago,

in which case
it will wait
quietly right
here until
you return

No Rush

There are some days
when no matter
what I say it feels
like I'm far away in
another country &
whoever is doing
the translating
has had far
too much
to drink

Lost in Translation

I can read minds,
she said & I said, OK
& she said, Do you
want to know what
you're thinking?

I said no thank you.

I don't do stuff like
that on weekends.

Down Time

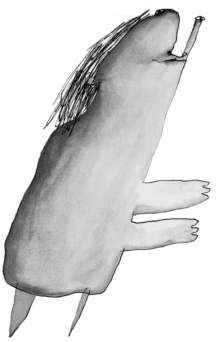

things have been
going so well
that she's taking
an anxiety break
to keep centered

Anxiety Break

I don't really
get jet lag, she
said. I just see
my husband's
failings more
clearly.

Side Effect

has always
been fascinated
by car crashes
& train wrecks,
so it's no
real surprise
how well
he took to
relationships

No Surprise

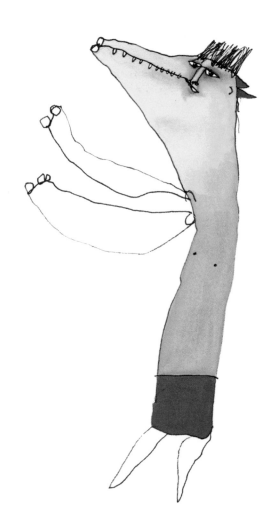

I need you
to come home
soon, she said.
I'm walking
around like
a woman who's
let herself go.

Aiming Low

**Hard to impress
because she's
already seen
the sun rise
today & it doesn't
get much better
than that.**

Hard to Impress

FAST TRACK

SLOW TRACK

REALLY SLOW TRACK

When I'm having
a really bad day,
she said,
I pretend I'm dead
& you'd be amazed
how much that
perks you
right up.

Make Believe

Can make stuff
magically disappear,
especially if it's
got a lot of butter
& sugar in it

Disappearing Act

won't drink a cheap red
no matter how much
they threaten him

Standards

That's the thing about free will, he told us. You can drag me along, but there's no way in hell you can make me have fun.

Free Will

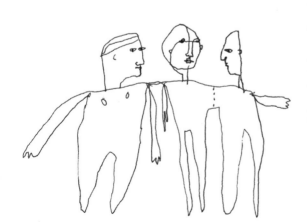

really wanting
to work up to
3 dimensions,
but not sure
it'll be as fun
as everyone says.

It's hard to trust
anyone who's already
doing it, he said.
They never remember
what they lost
to get there.

Innocence

Why is peace so
hard? she said
& I said peace
is easy.

Keeping our
mouths shut
is hard.

Hard Work

There's no incentive
to tell the truth
when you're already
in this deep, he said.

I'm just hoping
to die peacefully
in my sleep.

No Incentive

has some sort of disease
where you hallucinate &
start to not believe in love,
but after a year or two,
or even sometimes ten
or twenty, it cures itself
& all that's left are
a few little red spots
that twinge & ache
whenever you get
too near someone else
that has the disease
& it's all you can do
to stop from
reaching out &
holding them
close

Slow Cure

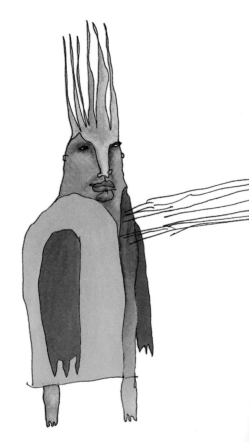

The children sat
in a circle around him
& he said, I don't believe
in life anymore
& no one said anything
for a while because
he was older than they
were & maybe knew
something they didn't,

but then someone said,
let's play a game &
someone said, Spy &
someone else said, Chase

& soon there was
no one there
but the man
sitting
alone

Circle Game

saving up
a bag full of
peak moments
she's going to have
someday if she can
ever get away
from all the
same old stuff
that's holding
her back

& you can pretty
well guess how
it's going

Saving Up

I was going
to live simply
& give away
all my money
to the poor,
she said, until
I figured out
then I'd be poor,
so the simple thing
was just to keep it.

I like it
when things
make sense
like that,
she added.

Simple Life

Sticking
his neck out
because he's
tired of just
sitting there
hoping people
will notice
him for his
calm energy

Tired of Sitting

little unclear on
how a sack race
actually works,
so he's got
a snowball's
chance in hell
of winning

Sack Race

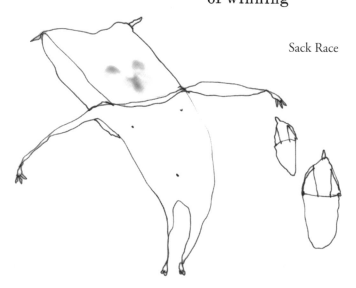

I only do this until I get dizzy
& then I lay down on my back &
watch the clouds, she said.

It sounds simple
but you won't believe
how many people
forget the second
part.

Proper Steps

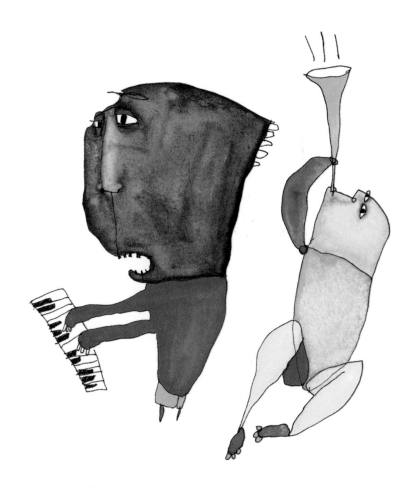

I'm not sure
if the world's
all that serious,
she said, or if
it just has
a really dark way
of having
a good time.

Dark Way

If you're right
& I'm not,
I'm going
to be hell
to live with,
she said.

So, you
better think
about that
next time
you want to
be right.

Being Right

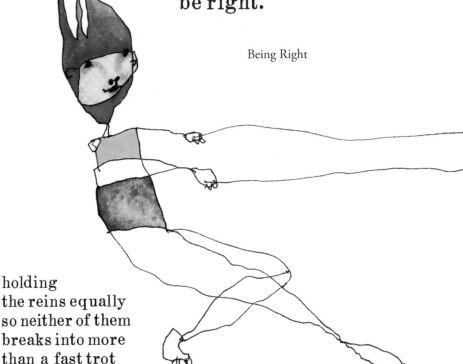

holding
the reins equally
so neither of them
breaks into more
than a fast trot

Fast Trot

Breakfast is not a competition, she said,

but they were gone already & both of them thought they'd won

Breakfast of Champions

When I grow up,
I want to remember
that I always wanted
to be about a thousand
different things
& one lifetime
didn't seem
nearly enough.

When I grow up,
I hope it's at
the very end
when it doesn't
matter any more
any way

Perfect Time

running wildly
into the spring
wind chasing
down all the
dandelions
before they
turn into just
weeds in a
couple of years

Just Weeds

Whatever you do,
she said, don't wait
too long or you'll
have to start from
the very beginning
& those new bodies
are always kind
of a crapshoot.

Crapshoot

If I get born again,
my son said,
do they give me
different parents?
& I said no & he
shook his head &
said they didn't
use their brains
on that one,
did they?

Born Again

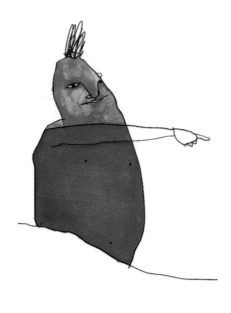

I'm not sure
if there's one
right place
I'm supposed
to be, he said,
but I know
a couple of
wrong places
I'd give a
second try
in a heartbeat.

Couple of Wrongs

I think they're
going to be great
grown-ups, she said,

because
they're
really
awful
children.

Present Tense

You seem very calm for a woman who's getting married, I said & she nodded. It's on my to-do list, she said, so there's no point in agonizing about it.

To-do List

It's taken me a long time to get here, he said, so I don't really care if it's wrong.

Solid Effort

Are we your real children? they said
& I said we had our pick
of all the children in the world, so
we took a few home to try out
& though we tried to
return them later,
it was more trouble
than it was worth,

so we kept them & loved them
& taught them all the stuff
they'd need to know
when it came time
for them to choose,
so they wouldn't make
the same mistakes we did

& later I heard one of them
say they didn't know
about being a parent
if it was as risky
as all that.

Calculated Risk

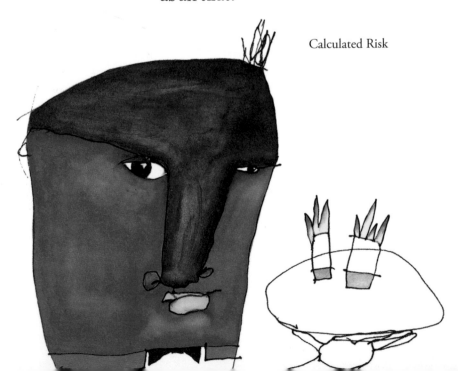

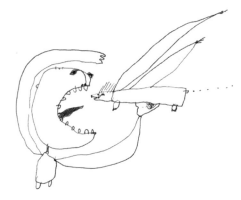

When did the world
go to hell? he said
& I said it happens
about this same time
every couple of years

& that seemed to
calm him down.

Clockwork

No one really
keeps score,
he said, but
if they did, we
would've won
5 to 2.

Knowing the Score

I don't have
many vices
beyond caring
what other
people think,
she said,

but that's
a big one.

Beyond Caring

If God had meant
for me to bend
like that, she said.
I would've been
born in India.

Birth Right

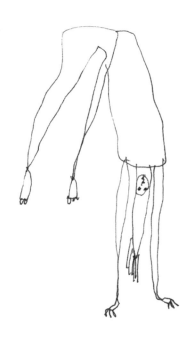

missing
a perfectly
good day because
she's sure that
she should be
anxious about
something

Perfectly Anxious

I will tell the truth
unless I get confused
& think I could
get in real trouble
if someone found out,
in which case,
I will lie as
convincingly
as possible for
as long as I
feel the need.

Promises to Myself

escaping as quickly
as they can from
a getaway weekend
gone bad

Getaway Weekend

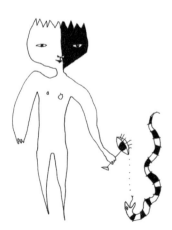

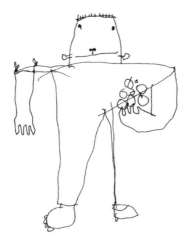

Frankenstein
bringing another pile
of fruit salad
to the potluck
because he's
all thumbs
in the kitchen.

All Thumbs

Of course I hang on
tight, she said.

You can't believe
the kind of stuff
that happens
when you let go.

Hanging on Tight

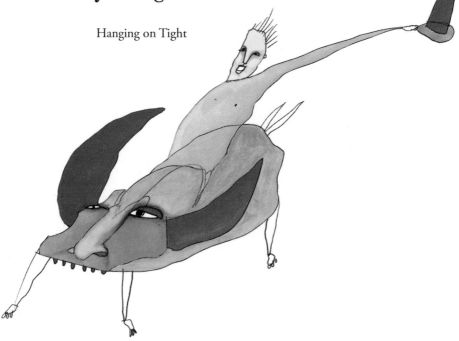

It would be
easier if I just
told the truth,
she said, but
I wasn't there
for a lot of it.

Tell the Truth

hiding his light
under a bushel
because he's been
priced out of
anything bigger
by this market

Hot Market

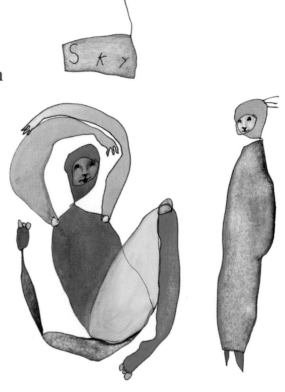

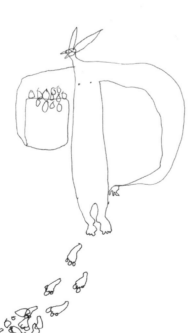

Start here
& go until
you die,
he said.
What's so
complicated
about that?

Straight Forward

The loss is not yours
alone, she said & you will
see it in their eyes
when they do not think
you are watching.

How long does it take?
I said & she put
her hand on my chest
& we did not speak.

Stand Still

They left me
with your shadow,
saying things like
Life is not fair

& I believed them
for a long time.

But today,
I remembered
the way you laughed
& the heat
of your hand
in mine

& I knew that
life is more fair
than we can
ever imagine
if
we are there
to live it.

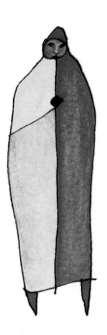

More Fair

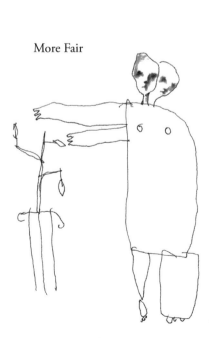

the water
washed away
everything but
the chance to
begin again

so we came
from cities & towns,
from long golden fields
& we stood side by side
until we made a bridge
to dry land,

back to a place
we have promised
to hold safe
for each other's
children,

back to a place
called home

Promise (After Katrina)

Wanting him
to come back
before anyone
notices a part
of the world
has not moved
since he left

Missing Piece

Sitting there in your pajamas
& all the time in the world &
if I could keep any moment
it would be this:

watching you & holding
my breath with the wonder
of it all.

The Wonder of It All

How can you be sure
it has a soul? she said.
You can't, I said,
unless you've got one
yourself.

Soul Mate

If I ran the world,
he told me, I'd
pretty much leave
it alone & spend
my time reading
& I'd advise other
people to do the same.

Which is why I'll
probably never run
the world, he said.

Benign Neglect

This holds a promise
to all the children
of the world, which
is how you can tell
it's the real dream
of America & not
one of those dreams
of fear & death that
glitter so brightly
on tv.

Real Dream

I promise you
not a moment
will be lost
as long as I have
heart & voice
to speak

& we will walk
again together
with a thousand
others & a thousand
more & on & on
until there is
no one among us
who does not
know the truth:

there is no future
without love.

Legacy

falling
back on
the classics
because it's easier
than admitting
all this modern
stuff is
a little bit
baffling

Classic Chic

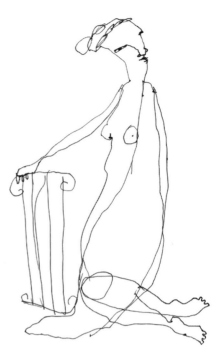

I've been doing these
Chinese stretches that
are supposed to make
you live longer, he told me.

I just hope I'm
not this sore
the whole time.

Stretching Out

this is a special
balancing trick
that requires
a small child
to stay
completely
still

(so it's still only
theoretical)

Good Trick

How hard is it to
make stuff up?
she said.
Not hard at all,
I said.

The real trick
is knowing to stop
before you get
confused.

Stopping Point

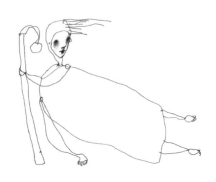

likes to navigate
by the stars even
when she's just
zipping over to
the mall

Star Gazer

This is a loose-fitting body, so it's still comfortable after a long carbohydrate binge.

Relaxed Fit

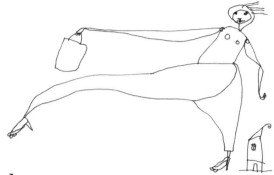

her only super powers
are that she can walk in
heels without wobbling

& if you don't think that's
amazing, you've obviously
never tried it.

Super Power

My grandfather
used to say
nobody
gives a damn
anymore

& the thing
I remember
most about him
is the way he
never let that
stop him from
giving a damn
all the days
of his life

Giving a Damn

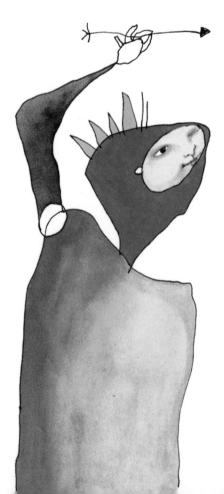

Counted up
all the things
she was afraid
of one night
& it took
so long she
fell asleep
from exhaustion

Dark Night

There are 2 things
I remember best,
she said. Beauty
& all the times
people insulted me,
so getting older
has been kind of
a roller-coaster
ride.

2 Things

keeps feeling
like he's being followed
by a cloud of insects,

but it's just
the relatives
watching

Insect Cloud

What are you doing? I said.
I'm invisible, he said, Do
I have to spell everything
out for you all the time?

& since he was invisible,
I decided I could ignore that.

Invisible

I'm going to get
as far away from you
as possible, she said,
& there's nothing
you can do
to stop me.

So, I shrugged
& turned & started
to walk away.

That's not fair,
she said,
you're not
even trying.

Full Effort

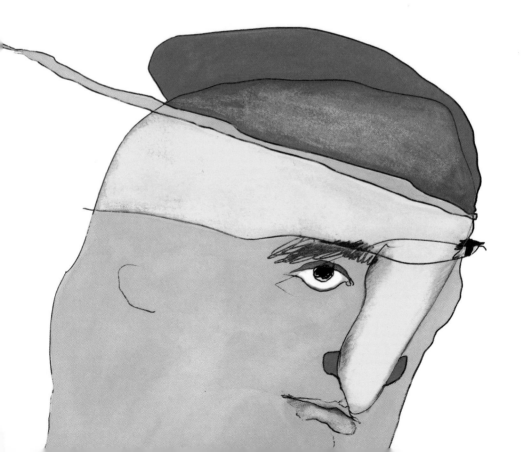

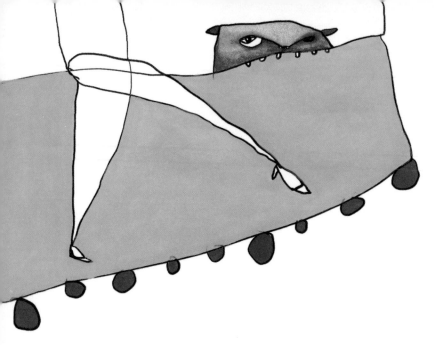

I'm trying to pack
for the future, he said,
but I think it's
too much stuff.

So what are you going
to do? I said.

& he shrugged
& said he was going
to trust that everything
would work out.

& he added, I'm moving
back in with my parents.

Future Plan

How do you start
a religion? he said.

I think you have faith
& then you wait for
a miracle, I said.
At least that's how
it's been done before.

He nodded. **OK,**
he said, so it's a lot
like e-commerce.

Start Up

**Tired of
knowing
everything
without ever
being sure**

Uncertainty Principle

I've never been
good about watching
my back because I'm too
worried about walking
into something &
breaking my nose
again.

Priorities

wondering if
Day of the Dead
is nine to five like all
the other dead days
he can remember

Regular Hours

I used to
live for the day,
she said, before
I moved to
Minnesota.

Now, I check
the temperature
before I do
anything.

Reserve Judgment

It took me
a long time,
she said, to
stop confusing
safety with love.

Confusion

Wrapped tightly
against a chill wind
she just remembered
from a long time ago

& no amount of
current time &
temperature can
help this one

Chill Wind

he followed
the sun & she
followed the stars
& in dreams they
listened closely
for the beginning
of all things, for
that was where
they knew they'd
find each other

Beginning

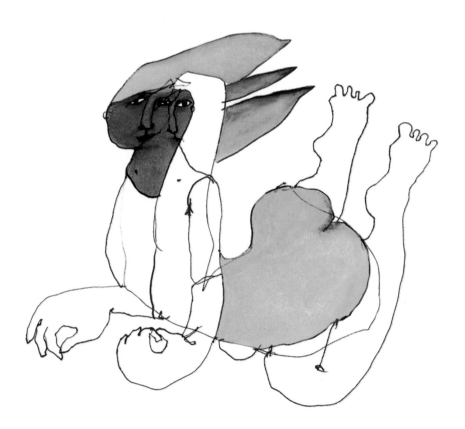

off on another
adventure of
a lifetime **&**
hoping he
won't forget
halfway
through
this time

Adventure of a Lifetime

If you were smart,
you'd probably spend
more time stretching,
he said

& I said, If I was really
smart, I'd probably
spend more time just
sitting in the shade
drinking lemonade

Smart Exercise

I think of it as
an opportunity
to find out how
much money means
to me, she said.

So far, it means
a lot more than
I think is probably
healthy.

Money Matters

I know
enough
to tell you
that fluff is a
substance too,
she said.

Material Girl

This is a
special container
for keeping lies
that you tell
yourself

& it doesn't let in
any light or air
otherwise they
start to go bad

& there's nothing
else you can do
but throw them out.

Special Container

We need a letter
that's like i & u
together for when
we're doing stuff
like this, he said
& I hugged him &
said a lot of people
want a letter like
that.

Perfect Combination

liking each other
because it's a beautiful
day & it seems like
a waste of time
to disagree about
stuff the other one
is refusing to change
out of sheer
stubbornness

Day Break

trapped mainly
by wanting things
to be exactly
as they are,

only better.

Better Trap

My favorite thing
is the wind, she said,

& my second
favorite is
chocolate

but I just do
that so I don't
get too skinny
& blow away

Favorite Things

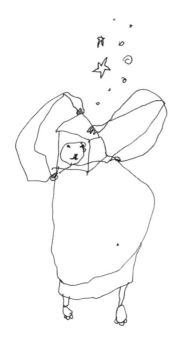

I still remember
the day the world
took you back &
kept you for her own
& there was never time
to thank you for
the thousand scattered
moments you left
behind to watch us
while we slept.

Thousand Moments

Only her skin
between her life
& a return to the
great wide ocean

Thin Skin

I carry you with me
into the world,
into the smell of the rain
& the words that dance
between people

& for me,
it will always
be this way,
walking in the light,
remembering being alive
together

Living Memory

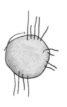

It came on her
without thinking
that she was
the exact age
as her mother was
& no matter what,
it would have
been hard to leave

& suddenly
all the generations
gathered around her
in that small kitchen
& held her close

& they would have
blocked the light
if they had not
come filled with
their memories
of love

Generations

When do you get to
be a grown-up? she said.

When you can
read & write & lie
without laughing,
I said

& her eyes got big &
she said she didn't
know it was that
hard

Big Job

This is one of those
rare bumblebees
who agreed with
the engineers about
not being able to fly

so he mainly
sits around
& watches
the other bees
work themselves
to death.

Design Flaw

I mainly want someone
to tell me I'm right &
then pay me, he said.
Is that too much to
ask?

& I said as long
as you're living
in a dream world,
you might as well
make it work
for you.

Dream World

Why is the world
so confusing? he said
& I said it's only
confusing if you
believe it has to
make sense
& he looked
at me & shook
his head.

I can't believe
they let just anyone
have children, he said.

Free Country

They only
look small,
she said,
if you're
someone
who's fond
of being
bigger
than
everyone
else.

Being Bigger

taunting the
neighbor's dog
with meat-flavored
tofu because he
can't get anyone
else to eat it.

Tofu Pup

I'm sick & tired of all these judgmental people, she said, & I hope they burn in hell for it.

Bitter End

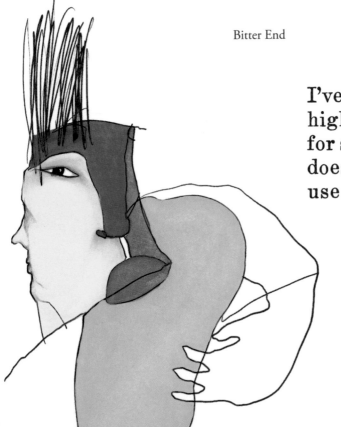

I've got pretty
high standards
for someone who
doesn't have any
use for them yet.

High Standards

I need to move
someplace where
Cheez Whiz isn't
a major food
group, she said.

Raising the Bar

I've found it's
best to leave
the hard moral
questions to them
what has hard
morals, he said.

Pirate Logic

What happened to
you? I said & she said
she was nurturing
the cat against its will

& that was the end
of that conversation.

Caregiver

I was thinking of either meditating or napping,

but the way I do it, there's not much difference except in the explanation to the rest of my family.

Flexible Practice

doesn't usually advise eating chocolate for breakfast unless you're absolutely convinced that's the kind of advice you need

Practical Advice

I like change,
she said, as long
as I remember
I like change.

Pep Talk

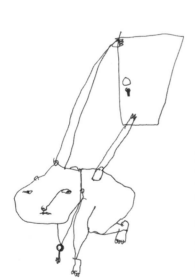

finally
has figured out
there aren't enough
quiet little British
films around to
protect her from
the real world

Quiet Little Films

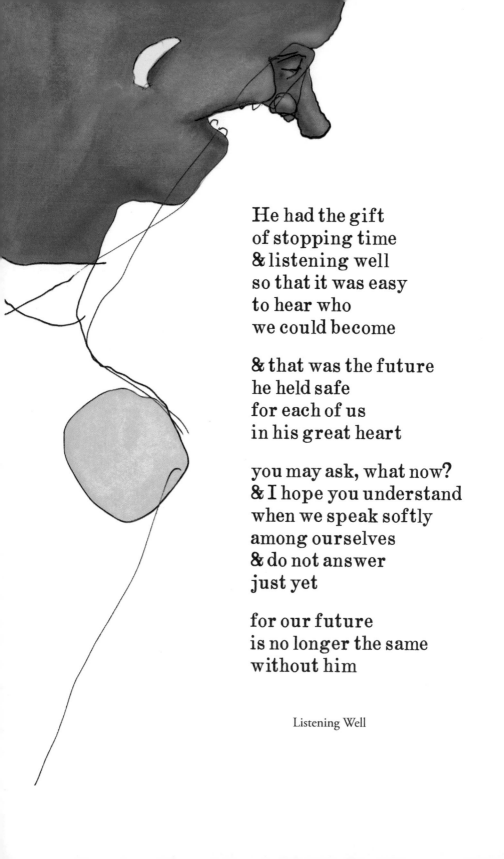

He had the gift
of stopping time
& listening well
so that it was easy
to hear who
we could become

& that was the future
he held safe
for each of us
in his great heart

you may ask, what now?
& I hope you understand
when we speak softly
among ourselves
& do not answer
just yet

for our future
is no longer the same
without him

Listening Well

There is no one
who comes here
that does not know
this is a true
map of the world,
with you there
in the center,
making home
for us all.

True Map

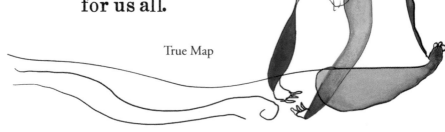

We're here to end it,
I said & she said, No,
we're here to begin it
& then she turned &
opened her arms
& everywhere I could see
there were people,
like bright birds, calling
with a thousand voices

& suddenly I understood.
Here is where it begins.
With all of us, together,
giving our children
a world worth loving
for a lifetime
to come.

Lifetime

In the heart of the world
there is a place that holds
the secret names
of the rocks & the trees
& all the children of the earth

& around it
gather women & men
who hold it dear
& each night
they stand together
to keep it safe
for as long as it takes
till morning comes

& no matter what
you have been told,
this will always be so,
in the heart of the world.

In the Heart of the World

About the Artist

I've been remembering the future through my art & stories since 1993. I suppose that doesn't make any sense. Remembering the future is my shorthand way of saying that we all have a hand in how the future turns out. The future I imagine for you & me & all the children of the world is one that's filled with laughter & music & love, played full out. It's the only thing that makes sense to me any more.

I came to this almost by accident. I've been a playwright, waiter, tennis player, chef, contract archaeologist, accountant, systems analyst & computer programmer, among other things. For a long time, I thought I'd be a famous marble sculptor, but I always wanted to explain what was going on in my pieces. I'd attach little explanations to them, or I'd surround them with stories. With very little regard for my future plans, people ignored my sculpture & just sat around reading the words. Fortunately, I figured out that I actually liked making up stories more than carving marble.

What else? We've raised two boys. We've travelled. We've moved cross-country several times. I collected a couple of degrees in there, too. I graduated from Luther College in Decorah, Iowa with a BA in various things & I've got an MFA in Fibre & Mixed Media (in case you think I'm just one of those popular artists who can't cut it in the real world of academia) from JFK University in Orinda, California.

After years of me whining about winter, we finally moved from Saint Paul, Minnesota, back to California. We've been here long enough already that I've started to complain when it gets down to the mid 50s at night. It's an old habit, but to tell you the truth, it's kind of hard to get worked up about winter when it means that only half as many flowers are blooming.

This is my eighth book. Of all the books, this feels most like my studio notebooks, with its mix of saturated color & quick black & white sketches. May it remind you of the joy of being alive on this wild planet...

About StoryPeople

StoryPeople has come to mean many things. StoryPeople can be the wood sculptures created by Brian Andreas. They can be one of the hundreds of his colorful story prints. They're the community of people on the web site who share their own stories as they make sense of the world we're making together & they're any of the hundreds of thousands of people worldwide who have come to know & love his work.

StoryPeople is also the name we give to the company of friends & co-workers who make it all possible. From our small town in Iowa, we distribute Brian Andreas' stories to galleries & bookstores all over the planet. We play with the web, imagining, almost daily, new ways to bring the stories to more people. We believe in the power of stories to transform our world & we believe now is the time, more than ever before. Our business is to give our world & ourselves tools to imagine & create & heal. Stories that cherish the quiet moments. Stories of a world that works for everyone. Stories about a world worth saving.

The sculptures, the prints & the books are available in galleries, gift stores & bookstores throughout the US, Canada & the EU (along with a few others scattered about the world) & on our web site. Please feel free to call, or write, for more information, or drop in on the web at **www.storypeople.com**

StoryPeople
P.O. Box 7
Decorah, IA 52101
USA

800.476.7178
563.382.8060
563.382.0263 FAX

orders@storypeople.com